Sejal Sinha

Swims with Sea Dragons

Also by Maya Prasad:

Sejal Sinha Battles Superstorms

Sejal Sinha

Swims with Sea Dragons

BY MAYA PRASAD ★ ILLUSTRATED BY ABIRA DAS

ALADDIN

New York London Toronto Sydney New Delhi

ALADDIN

An imprint of Simon & Schuster Children's Publishing Division
1230 Avenue of the Americas, New York, New York 10020
First Aladdin hardcover edition October 2023
Text copyright © 2023 by Maya Prasad
Illustrations copyright © 2023 by Abira Das
Also available in an Aladdin paperback edition.
All rights reserved, including the right of reproduction in whole or in part in any form.
ALADDIN and related logo are registered trademarks of Simon & Schuster, Inc.
For information about special discounts for bulk purchases, please contact
Simon & Schuster Special Sales at 1-866-506-1949 or business@simonandschuster.com.
The Simon & Schuster Speakers Bureau can bring authors to your live event. For more information or to book an event contact the Simon & Schuster Speakers Bureau at 1-866-248-3049 or visit our website at www.simonspeakers.com.
Designed by Heather Palisi
The illustrations for this book were rendered digitally.
The text of this book was set in Berling Nova Text Pro.
Manufactured in the United States of America 0923 BVG
2 4 6 8 10 9 7 5 3 1
CIP data for this book is available from the Library of Congress.
ISBN 9781665911818 (hc)
ISBN 9781665911801 (pbk)
ISBN 9781665911825 (ebook)

For my husband—
and our boundless adventures
—M. P.

For Mummum and Babai for letting me be
myself, wild and free like the sea!
—A. D.

 CONTENTS

Sejal Sinha
Swims with Sea Dragons

CHAPTER ONE
Glitter Bomb

The best part about school projects is definitely the glitter.

I was working on a poster for my ocean creatures presentation on the dining room table, and I added another dash of red glitter, just to make the tummy of my immortal jellyfish look extra bright.

"Can I help?" asked my five-year-old little brother, Abu.

"No way," I said. "This needs to be perfect."

Abu made a pouty face, and then snatched the glitter bottle.

"Stay away!" I said.

He got an evil-little-brother look. The next thing I knew, a glitter bomb exploded all over us!

Our cookies-and-cream-colored Havanese puppy, Fluff Monster, yapped and ran in circles in the cloud of red sparkles. It got all over her fur. All over my hair. All over Abu the most. He looked like he was made of sparkly fire.

Mom came in to see what Fluff Monster was barking about. She took one look at Abu, and just shook her head. I waited for her to get super mad but instead she laughed. "New look you're trying out?"

Abu grinned and twirled. "Yeah, do I look good?"

"Very good," Mom said. But she also fixed him with a stern look and held out her hand.

He stopped twirling and gave her the glitter shaker.

"Thank you," Mom said.

I rolled my eyes because it seemed like Abu never got into trouble for anything. But Mom would probably yell at me for making a mess on the table.

She came over to look at my poster. "Wow, Sejal! Your project is coming out so nicely. I wish I could live forever like the immortal jellyfish!"

Phew. She was smiling at least. Maybe her latest experiments at her science lab had been going well or something.

"Sorry about the mess on the dining table," I said, "but Fluff Monster kept stealing my markers when I tried to work on it in the basement."

I loved Fluff, but she could definitely be naughty sometimes. And she really liked stealing anything that was stick-shaped, like pencils or markers. The dining table was too high for her to reach, though.

Mom rubbed my shoulders. "It's okay. Not like we're expecting anyone today."

"Nope, just a normal evening!" Dad said cheerfully from the kitchen. "We can eat dinner on the kitchen island."

I noticed he was wearing his favorite frilly apron and was stirring a big pot with lots of steam coming out. Something smelled good, but I'd been so busy working on my project that I hadn't paid attention until right now.

Just then, Fluff Monster started barking at the front door.

CHAPTER TWO
Pet Penguins

Do you want to see who it is?" Mom asked.

I shrugged. "Maybe they're just delivering the mail really late?"

Fluff had great hearing and always knew when someone was on the porch. It was usually just a postal worker, though.

"Woof! Woof! Woof!" Fluff Monster barked some more.

Then the doorbell rang, so I guessed it wasn't just regular mail. Maybe a package?

"Go on," said Mom.

She had a goofy grin on her face. So did Dad. I didn't know why they were being so mysterious, but I went to the door.

When I saw Neela Phua's smiling face through the window, I screamed in delight and dropped the marker I was holding. Of course Fluff Monster snatched it right up, but I couldn't care about that when my awesome aunt was here. I hadn't seen her in months!

I pulled the door open and leaped into my aunt's arms. "Neela Phua! You're back from Antarctica?"

"Just got home yesterday." She squeezed me back and plopped a wet kiss onto my forehead. "I thought it would be fun to surprise you."

"Did you bring me a pet penguin?" I asked.

Neela Phua laughed and gently put me back on the ground. "You know that our motto is to leave living creatures in their natural habitats."

"So you didn't bring me even one little baby penguin?" I peeked inside the top of her purse. Nope, no penguins in there.

"Sorry, dear," Neela Phua said. "There weren't any gift shops at our station either. Only other scientists like me were there."

Abu ran over to give Neela Phua a big hug also. Then he puffed out his chest. "I'm going to be a famous scientist when I grow up too. And all the penguins will be my friends."

My family was full of scientists. My mom was an astrophysicist (studying stars and planets). My dad worked in neuroscience (stuff about brains). And Neela Phua, Dad's sister, was a marine biologist. I had a ton of other aunts and uncles who did science-y stuff, too.

Neela Phua patted Abu's head. "That sounds lovely. And I suppose you're still planning to be an adventurer, Sejal?"

I nodded. "Science is cool, but there are enough scientists in this family already. I want to go out and explore things and see the whole world! Maybe even the whole universe!"

"Sounds like an excellent plan," Neela Phua said.

"Mmf! Mmf!" squeaked Fluff Monster. She wanted Neela Phua's attention even though she still had my stolen marker in her mouth.

"I missed you too, Fluff." My aunt scratched her behind the ears. "So, Sejal, where has that cardboard box you love so much taken you recently? Any more treasure hunting or trips to the moon?"

I grinned at her. "Well, we did fly into a hurricane . . ."

CHAPTER THREE
Weird but Cool

When we walked back to the dining room, my parents had put away my project supplies, and the table now had a bunch of delicious-looking (and smelling) food on it.

"So much for eating around the kitchen island!" I said.

Dad winked at me as he pulled out a chair for Neela Phua. "Well, since we have a surprise guest, I thought maybe the table would be better."

I could tell he was joking and that he'd known

all along that Neela Phua was coming. But it really was a good surprise, since she was such a fun aunt. Besides, Dad had made my favorite catfish curry dish. Yum.

Neela Phua closed her eyes and sniffed. "Oh my, I missed Indian food so much! This smells amazing."

As she piled up her plate, Dad made one for me, and Mom made one for Abu. Fluff Monster finally dropped my slobbered-on marker to sniff around under the table. There wasn't anything to lick up yet, but I'd be sure to drop a bit of rice for her.

Mom lit the candles. "What's life like in Antarctica, Neela?"

"Very cold," said Neela Phua. "So cold that we have to be really careful. If you even drop your mitten, you could get frostbite on your hand. It's not an easy place to be."

"How do animals live there, then?" I asked.

"They've adapted to the cold," Neela Phua said as she scooped up some fish curry with her poori.

She had a bit of spicy yellow sauce on her chin, but she didn't seem to care. She ate like she hadn't had anything good for months. "Penguins have feathers that keep them warm. The fish there have special proteins to keep their bodies from freezing. But we humans don't. Honestly, I could use a trip to the beach!"

I snuck Fluff Monster a little bit of poori under the table. I knew she wasn't supposed to have too much human food, but it was a very tiny piece. "Maybe you can help teach Fluff how to swim. She's scared of the water."

Neela Phua smiled. "That sounds fun. Now, your mom told me you have a big presentation tomorrow?"

I nodded. "Yes. I just hope Jonah doesn't ask any questions about it."

"Who's Jonah?" Neela Phua asked.

"He's a boy in my class," I said sourly. Even thinking about him made me feel like I was sucking on a lemon. "He always calls me weird. He thinks everything I do is weird."

"'Weird' is just another word for 'cool,'" Neela Phua said, patting my hand. "There are some very weird—and cool—creatures in the ocean! Like barreleye fish. They have a clear head that looks like the windshield of a submarine, and their eyes are big green round balls that face up inside their heads. They can actually look in different directions."

"Weird," I said.

"And cool," Neela Phua added.

Okay, she had a point. Weird could definitely be cool. But did Jonah know that?

CHAPTER FOUR
Wild Genius Cheetah

*K*ABOOM!

"What was that?" I grabbed at the table as the house shook.

"What was what?" Mom said, as if she'd missed the sound of an explosion.

BLAM!

"Ahhh!" Abu screamed. Then he laughed. He liked to scream, for the fun of it.

"What are you two going on about?" Dad asked.

Mom shrugged. "Must be some game they're playing."

"Oh, that makes sense," Neela Phua said, continuing to enjoy her catfish curry.

I stared at them. How could they not feel the house rocking and shaking as if there were an earthquake? Grown-ups were so strange.

But Fluff Monster had her ears perked up. "Arf! Arf! Arf!"

She ran to the basement door. I dashed after her, Abu right behind me.

"I guess they're done with dinner," Mom said.

"Have fun, kids!" Neela Phua called.

Fun? I wasn't sure if whatever was happening in the basement would be fun. But I wasn't surprised when I saw Professor Cheetah with smoking tools, her whiskers twitching.

Professor Cheetah was the smartest and best of all my stuffies, but she never let grown-ups see her master designs. Right now she was holding up my toy tuba—but she'd converted it into some strange instrument with lots of controls and displays all over it.

"My invention works!" she purred.

"What did you make now?" I came closer to look at it.

"It's a Micromaker," Professor Cheetah said. "It can shrink things to any size. Look—I converted the Snack Pack!"

She indicated with her paw that we should look into her microscope. Sure enough, when I peeked through the lens, I saw a tiny shrunken thing that had to be the Snack Pack. It was a special backpack that Professor Cheetah had invented, and it held a lot more stuff than an ordinary backpack. Practically our whole pantry fit inside that backpack.

"Let me see!" Abu insisted, poking me with his elbow. "Oh no! My string cheese is tiny! And we don't have any more."

"We just had a giant dinner," I pointed out.

Professor Cheetah sniffed my breath. "Did you have catfish curry?"

"If you're hungry, maybe you shouldn't have shrunk the Snack Pack," I reminded her. "Which had your impala-flavored chips."

"And gazelle jerky," Abu added. "How do you unshrink it?"

Professor Cheetah's whiskers twitched. "Well, that's the problem. I need an energy source for the Unshrinker. Something really powerful."

I rolled my eyes. "Why didn't you think of that before shrinking the snacks?"

"I thought a simple battery would work . . . but then I realized I did the math wrong. One little mistake in carrying the three—and, well . . ." Professor Cheetah shrugged.

"My string cheese . . ." Abu whined.

Even Fluff Monster whimpered, like she knew her favorite biscuits had also been shrunk.

"Wonderful," I said. "Well, I can't help you right now. I need to finish my ocean project."

Professor Cheetah flicked her tail. "Well, can you at least sneak me some catfish curry?"

CHAPTER FIVE
Immortal Jellyfish

On Friday, I finally gave my big presentation. Neela Phua had helped me practice the night before, so even though I usually got nervous speaking in front of the class, I felt like I knew my stuff.

When Mrs. Drake called on me, I grabbed my poster and propped it on the marker tray of the big whiteboard. Now everyone could see my chart with the life stages of the immortal jellyfish.

"The *Turritopsis dohrnii* is sometimes called

the immortal jellyfish," I said to the class. "That's because it can live forever. It can die if a bigger predator eats it, but if it's only hurt, it can heal itself."

I pointed to the life-cycle pictures. The jellyfish started as a cell, then grew into something called polyps before finally reaching the medusa stage. That was when it actually looked like a jellyfish, with a big round head and long tentacles.

"If the jellyfish is hurt," I said, "the medusa can turn back into little cells and start its life all over again. It can turn back into a baby."

The class seemed impressed.

"I wish I could do that!" Marianna exclaimed.

Mrs. Drake said, "Please raise your hand if you have something to say."

Jonah raised his hand. He had a grin on his face, and I knew he was going to say something annoying. But Mrs. Drake called on him anyway.

"Yes, do you have a question, Jonah?"

"Yep," Jonah said. "Where in the bottom of the sea did your parents find you?"

Some of the kids in my class laughed, but at least my friends Sara and Rashmi didn't.

"Jonah!" Mrs. Drake pursed her lips. "That was very rude. I want you to apologize to Sejal."

"I'm sorry you're so weird," Jonah said.

Remembering Neela Phua's words, I retorted, "Weird is cool, actually. Just like this immortal jellyfish."

"Sure it is," he said, smirking.

Mrs. Drake told him to apologize again, so he rolled his eyes and said, "Sorry."

I didn't believe he was even a teensy bit actually sorry, but I tried not to let him bother me.

"He's just a horrible boy," Sara whispered after my presentation.

"Super-stinky horrible," Rashmi agreed.

I was glad for my friends, but Jonah had still pretty much ruined my Friday.

CHAPTER SIX
Fluff Monster versus the Swim Toy

On Saturday, my family went to the beach. I was excited because we were meeting a bunch of my aunts and uncles and cousins there—and I'd get to spend more time with Neela Phua. She'd been gone for so many months in Antarctica, and I was glad she could finally play with me.

"Will you help me teach Fluff Monster how to swim?" I asked her. "I keep trying, but Fluff never goes in the water."

"Sure," said Neela Phua. "Let's go."

As my parents and aunts and uncles settled our stuff at a picnic table, Fluff Monster brought me her doggie life vest.

"She seems excited about swimming," Neela Phua said.

"For some reason she likes me to put the vest on." I buckled and zipped it so it was snug around her. "But she still doesn't want to get in the water. Even when I throw this for her."

I held up a special toy. It was red and sparkly and made crinkly noises when I squeezed it.

"Arf! Arf! Arf!" Fluff Monster wagged her tail. She loved the toy.

We walked across the sand to get closer to the water. Fluff Monster pranced at my feet, barking excitedly.

I threw the toy, and it floated on the gentle waves. Fluff Monster ran to the edge of the sand. And then she just stopped. Her nose twitched as she smelled the salty ocean water.

"Go fetch!" I pointed to the toy.

But Fluff just lay down on the sand instead.

"See?" I said. "She won't go."

Neela Phua got the toy from the water and tried to tempt Fluff Monster. "Be a good pup! Go fetch!" She squeezed the toy to make the crinkling noise a few times, and then tossed it into the water, but not very far.

Fluff twitched her nose. The toy was so close to the beach that the waves pushed it onto the sand. Fluff wagged her tail excitedly and fetched it.

"See? She didn't swim!" I said.

"Yes, but we're just trying to get her comfortable with the water," Neela Phua explained. "She'll swim when she's ready."

Fluff offered her the toy, and Neela Phua tossed it for her again. Just as before, Fluff waited for the waves to push the toy back onto the sand. Then she picked it up and pranced around as if she were very proud of herself.

"Maybe it would help if you and Abu were swimming," Neela Phua suggested. "Then she'd see that it's fun and that the water feels good."

"It *is* fun!" said Abu. He took a running start,

leaped into the water, and then somersaulted in the waves.

"Woo-hoo!" I yelled, following him. I dived under the surface and kicked hard with my legs.

When I came up for air, I splashed Abu. He splashed me back. Then we snuck up on Neela Phua and splashed her.

"Ack!" she said. "Actually, that feels good. The water is so nice and warm here. Not like in Antarctica."

Fluff Monster barked from the sand, but still wouldn't get in.

"Ooh, what's that?" Abu said. He was looking at something in the shallow water a little bit farther down the beach.

Fluff Monster's ears perked up. She ran up near Abu, and even went into the water—just a little bit. She started growling at whatever he was looking at like she did when the postal worker came to our door. She definitely thought it was suspicious!

"What did you find?" Neela Phua asked.

We both dashed over. A strange-looking creature was floating in the water. It was only about an inch long, and it looked a little slimy but also really beautiful. It was bright blue and white, with four legs that each had long feathery fingers. Its tail had more of the feathery fingers, and the head had two little slimy horns. The neck had two more horns.

Abu reached out to touch it.

"Stop!" Neela Phua shouted.

CHAPTER SEVEN
Real Dragons

Abu quickly pulled his hand back. Neela Phua wasn't the kind of grown-up who usually yelled at kids, so when she did, we knew it was serious.

"Don't touch it," she said. "That's a blue dragon."

Abu's eyes widened. So did mine.

"A dragon?" Abu asked.

Neela Phua took Abu's sand bucket and, without touching the creature, used the opening to scoop the blue dragon inside along with some water. "It's actually a type of sea slug."

"'Dragon' sounds a lot cooler than 'sea slug,'" I said.

Neela Phua chuckled. "Yes, I suppose it does. But this dragon might be very venomous."

"Venomous?" Abu asked. "What's that?"

"It means it has toxins that can hurt you."

"So it's poisonous!" Abu said.

"Well, scientists call creatures poisonous if you get sick when you eat them, but venomous creatures are ones that release toxins when they bite you or sting you. The funny thing about blue dragons is that they aren't venomous on their own. They can become venomous depending on what they eat. Their favorite snack is called a Portuguese man-of-war, which is kind of like a jellyfish but it drifts on top of the ocean. Man-of-wars are much larger than blue dragons, but somehow the little guys manage to eat them anyway. And when they do, the man-of-war's toxic stinging cells don't hurt the blue dragon. Instead blue dragons can absorb the toxic stinging cells right into their tiny little cerata."

"Cerata?" I asked.

"Those things that look like fingers," she said, pointing. "If you touch them, you could get stung! It's very dangerous."

Abu sulked. "But it's so pretty. Can't I just pet it quickly?"

"No," Neela Phua said sternly. "Actually, sea slugs are often very pretty. Lots of bright colors. Blue dragons have their blue color to camouflage with the water surface. They float on their backs and drift over the ocean. We need to find a way to get this little guy back out there."

I looked at the blue dragon. Who knew something so tiny could be so fierce? I thought it was really cool that they could take the man-of-war's stinging power and use it for themselves.

If only I could do that at school. If only I could steal Jonah's power to make me so mad! I would love to turn the tables on him sometime. I knew teasing wasn't nice, but didn't he deserve it?

I glanced back at the small fierce creature. "I think we should give it a name."

"Well, I get to choose since I found it!" Abu said. "How about Blue Boss?"

"Hmm, actually that is pretty good," I admitted. I especially liked how Blue Boss was both beautiful and tough. It didn't have to be just one thing.

Just then, I heard someone saying, "Jonah! Jonah! Come have some lunch!"

I hoped that maybe it was some other Jonah, not Jonah Williams. Not the one who spent his time at school calling me "weird."

Please let it be some other Jonah.

But no, there he was. Running across the sand right toward us.

He smiled at me like we were friends. "Hey, Sejal."

"Um, hi." I picked up Professor Cheetah, who I'd left sitting on a driftwood log. She was ferocious and would protect me, I was sure of it. I gave her our secret signal to eat whoever I was talking to.

But Professor Cheetah just flicked her tail. That meant she wasn't in the mood to eat my enemy.

"You brought your stuffed animal to the beach?" Jonah smirked.

I really needed to be like Blue Boss and be able to steal his smirk.

"Ooh, what's that?" he asked, noticing the bucket. He reached out to touch the blue dragon.

"Stop!" I yelled at the same time that Abu and Neela Phua both shouted, "No!"

Fluff Monster barked a warning too. Even though Jonah was annoying and horrible and had ruined my presentation on Friday, I wasn't going to let him get stung. That would be too mean.

Maybe I didn't want his powers after all. I just wanted to be myself.

"What? I wasn't going to hurt it." Jonah looked surprised.

Jonah's mom ran over to join us.

"Jonah, I told you it was time for some lunch," she scolded him. The she noticed Blue Boss in the bucket. "Oh, what in the world is that?"

Neela Phua started explaining about the blue dragon—and how venomous it could be.

"But it's so small," said Jonah. "How could it hurt you?"

"Trust me," Neela Phua said. "Even though it's small, the toxins in its sting can be mighty."

Now my mom and dad had also come down to see what the fuss was about. Soon my other aunts and uncles joined too.

"Ah, I remember seeing a nature show about these!" Dad said. "I think it's rare for them to wash up on shore around here like this."

Sheela Mausi adjusted her reading glasses. "Let me look them up on my phone. Oh yes, the blue dragon, a member of the sea slug family . . ."

My relatives were definitely going into scientist-family mode. They got excited about cool science stuff, and even I thought the blue dragon was the coolest.

"Your family is so weird," Jonah said.

"They're awesome and smart," I retorted.

"They're so loud," Jonah said.

Sure, when my family got excited, they talked a lot. So what?

I narrowed my eyes at him. Maybe I should have let Blue Boss sting him after all.

CHAPTER EIGHT
Imagination Fuel

The grown-ups discussed how to get Blue Boss out to the open ocean and far enough from shore that the creature wouldn't end up drifting right back to the beach. I tried to tell them I had a plan for that, but grown-ups almost never believed that kids could get anything important done.

So I ignored them and turned to Professor Cheetah. "Hey, why didn't you eat Jonah when I signaled?"

"Little boys give me tummy troubles," she whispered back, flicking her tail.

"Whatever." I rolled my eyes. "I think we should make our own boat and return Blue Boss to the open ocean ourselves!"

Professor Cheetah's whiskers twitched, as they did when she was getting one of her brilliant ideas. "How about a submarine? Because I think I know where we can get some powerful energy to unshrink the Snack Pack!"

"Huh? Where?" I asked.

"You'll see." Professor Cheetah stuck out her fuzzy chest. "I'm brilliant."

"And not very humble," I muttered.

"Cheetahs don't need to be humble," she said.

"There's just one problem," I said. "We didn't bring a cardboard box."

Cardboard box magic is a powerful thing. We had all our best adventures in them. But I hadn't thought to bring one to the beach.

Professor Cheetah put on her safety goggles. "Don't worry, driftwood logs have plenty of the same magic as cardboard boxes, as long as you power them with Imagination Fuel."

"Imagination Fuel?" I said. "Are you sure?"

"Believe me." She flicked her tail like her usual know-it-all self. "Driftwood logs are an excellent substitute. We also have plenty of raw materials. Look—stones, shells, water, sand, mud."

I shook her paw, suddenly excited for another one of our adventures. "Let's do this!"

Professor Cheetah used empty seashells to create the engine—after checking that no creatures were still living inside, of course. (We wouldn't want any more little guys to lose their homes.) Next I found some seaweed and twigs for the steering wheel and rudder. Even Abu helped out, making all the buttons we would need for the control panel with little rocks. Last, I poured some seawater mixed with Imagination Fuel into the engine.

The log started transforming into a big yellow submarine right in front of our eyes. It was so beautiful, and I couldn't wait to take it out into

the ocean! Abu, Professor Cheetah, and I pushed
it into the water so only the periscope was sticking out. I'd read about submarines for my ocean
project too. The periscope looked like a telescope,
and we'd be able to use it to see above the water
once we were inside the submarine.

We climbed in through a hatch on the top. Abu managed to hold the bucket with Blue Boss as he climbed down the ladder inside. I carried Fluff Monster, who was wiggling in my arms.

At the back of the submarine, diving suits were hung up on a rack. It looked like there was some kind of robot there too. Along the side were small round windows where fish swished by. In the front, there was another round window above a fancy control panel, and a big steering wheel.

Professor Cheetah grabbed it. "I'm driving this time."

"No way! I'm in charge," I said. "It was my idea."

"But do you even know the way to the nearest hydrothermal vent? We need to get my special unshrinking power source," Professor Cheetah said in her usual bossy way.

"What?" I said. "We're not going to some hydrothermal vent right now—whatever that is! We have to get Blue Boss home."

"Hydrothermal vents are cracks in the bottom

of the ocean where hot water and minerals come bursting out because the area gets heated up by magma underneath the seafloor. A lot of energy comes out of those vents!" Professor Cheetah explained in her bossy know-it-all voice.

I was used to her being a know-it-all, but right now I wasn't really interested in these vent things. I just wanted to get Blue Boss home.

"Sounds dangerous," I said. "Not that I'm afraid or anything."

Professor Cheetah's tail flicked. "You're right— it's dangerous to go that deep for regular human grown-ups, and we could get hit with really hot water and chemicals if a vent bursts right beneath us. But our submarine is obviously stronger and better than any regular submarine. It's the perfect way to get the amount of power we need to unshrink the Snack Pack."

"Snacks are very important," Abu added. "Plus, would visiting these scary vent things make us famous? Because I want to be famous!"

It did sound cool. But I was on a completely different mission at the moment, in case they'd forgotten.

"You're not getting famous!" I told Abu. "And unshrinking the Snack Pack is not as important as getting poor Blue Boss home safely!"

I yanked the submarine wheel one way, and Professor Cheetah yanked the other way. Fluff Monster got all excited because of our fighting. Just then I heard someone else climbing down the ladder.

"Arf! Arf! Arf!" Fluff Monster barked.

I blinked.

Jonah was in the submarine! How had he found us? But I didn't have time to ask because I was still fighting over the steering wheel with Professor Cheetah. From the corner of my eye, I saw Jonah pick up Professor Cheetah's Micro-maker.

"What's this?" he asked. "And how did you make this submarine?"

"Put that down!" I said, yanking at the steering wheel again.

"Yes, please be careful with that," Professor Cheetah added, yanking back.

I wasn't sure which one of us did it, but suddenly the submarine started moving forward. Really fast. Jonah stumbled, dropping the Micromaker.

KABLAM!

There was an explosion. And the next thing I knew, the steering wheel was getting bigger and bigger. Soon I couldn't hold on to it anymore because it was too huge for my hands. I let go, and felt something weird happening in my body. Like all my body parts were getting squished into a sock.

"What the heck?" I shouted. "What's going on?"

"Ahh!" Jonah screamed.

Professor Cheetah made an odd mewling noise, and Abu was screaming too.

That's when I realized—the steering wheel hadn't gotten bigger. We were all getting smaller!

The Micromaker must have hit us. I spotted Professor Cheetah's new invention rolling across the submarine and crashing into the robot.

BLAM!

CHAPTER NINE
Six Inches Tall

After the second explosion there was good news and there was bad news. The good news: the diving suits had also gotten shrunk. The bad news: we were all less than six inches tall!

The blast must have missed Fluff Monster because she was still her regular size. She was a small dog, but now she was twice my height. She gave me a big wet lick.

"Yuck!" I felt like I'd just taken a shower in drool.

"Well, at least my instrument is working quite well," Professor Cheetah said.

Jonah's eyes were wide. "This can't really be happening!"

Fluff Monster gave him a big lick too. What a traitor! But at least now I wasn't the only one showered in dog drool.

"Ewww!" Jonah moaned.

"This is puurrrfect," Professor Cheetah purred. "Now we have even more reason to visit the hydrothermal vents! If you ever want to return to our regular size, that is!"

I glared at Jonah. "This is all your fault. Why'd you come in here anyway?"

He scratched his head. "It looked cool?"

"You mean weird?"

He just shrugged and glanced around. Blue Boss's bucket was still okay, thankfully, on the side of the dashboard. If the blue dragon's sting was dangerous to a full-size human, I couldn't imagine what it would feel like now. Not good.

Now that we were tiny, the round windows

were a lot higher than us, but we could still see outside. When the Micromaker had gone off, we must have zoomed pretty far out into the Atlantic Ocean, because we definitely weren't near the shore anymore.

We were speeding along, still near the surface of the ocean. There was lots of sunlight showing through the water, and it made so many pretty colors. Greens and blues and golds and turquoise and teal and everything in between. All sorts of interesting creatures were swimming around out there: jellyfish, stingrays, dolphins, a bunch of different kinds of pretty fish. A sea turtle swam by, and it seemed like its flippers were waving hi at us.

"Getting shrunk is kind of weird," Jonah said. "But this is also pretty cool!"

I glared at him, just in case he was about to say something mean like he usually did at school. But it seemed like he really was having fun. He was already here, so I might as well try to get along with him. I stuck out my hand. "Welcome to the SS *Fluff*."

CHAPTER TEN
Mission Unshrink Ourselves

Professor Cheetah's whiskers twitched. "Come on, let's get going to the hydrothermal vents. We'll get the Unshrinker working in no time— unless you want to take dog-drool showers every day."

Abu shrugged. "It's not so bad. Fluff Monster's drool is kinda warm."

"Ugh!" I said, wrinkling my nose. "Gross. Fine, we'll go to your vent thingies! It's not like we can take Blue Boss home like this. We can't even lift the bucket! How will we get to the control panel?" I pointed up at it.

Professor Cheetah considered. "Maybe Fluff Monster can help us with something other than dog-drool showers." She called for Fluff to come and sit.

Fluff Monster decided to be a very good puppy, and did not seem to mind as Professor Cheetah and I climbed on top of her.

"Hey, what about us?" Abu complained.

"We'll be too heavy for her with four people," I said. Sure, we'd shrunk, but Fluff was still a small dog.

"Come on, this way," I coaxed, trying to get Fluff to go to the control panel.

Fluff pranced around. She had no idea what I wanted her to do. Instead she sniffed around all over the submarine. First she sniffed the diving suits that had also been shrunk. Then she investigated the Micromaker dropped in the corner. Finally she came to the robot. It had two metal legs and ten metal arms. Its eyes were small cameras. It had a speaker for a mouth.

"What's the robot for?" I asked Professor Cheetah.

Abu and Jonah came to look too.

Professor Cheetah's whiskers twitched. "I call her Durga, because she has many arms like the Hindu goddess."

"Why does the robot need ten arms?" Jonah asked.

"So she can do ten things at once, of course," Professor Cheetah said. "She'll be able to collect what I need for the Unshrinker since we can't dive there ourselves."

"Why not?" Abu pouted. "I want to go scuba diving!"

"Because," Professor Cheetah said, "like I said before, the hydrothermal vents are too deep for us to dive to. There's so much water above that it can crush our bones. There's also really hot stuff exploding out of the ground—and you can't predict exactly when it will happen."

Yikes. That definitely didn't sound good.

Fluff Monster finally trotted over to the control panel.

"Thanks for the ride!" I said as Professor Cheetah and I scrambled off her back and up onto the dash.

Now we could look out the big window in the front. It hadn't been very big before we'd gotten shrunk. According to Professor Cheetah, submarines were stronger if the windows were smaller. But now that we were shrunken, the window was twice my size. I hopped onto the sill and felt like I was inside a giant aquarium.

"Excellent. Now let's see, where are we exactly?" Professor Cheetah started pushing buttons by pouncing on them. They were too big now to press with just one paw. "Good thing this sub has smart safety technology that will prevent us from running into islands or other continents. Hmmm, we're already near the shore of Australia? Imagination Fuel works a lot faster than normal fuel, I guess."

Just then Jonah and Abu catapulted off Fluff Monster's back onto the control panel too.

"Woo-hoo!" yelled Jonah, flapping his arms.

"Booyah!" screamed Abu as they both landed beside us.

I put my hands on my hips. "We're trying to navigate this thing. It's serious business."

"Uh-huh. . . ." Jonah's eyes got really wide, and he pointed out the front window. "Whoa. Is that a DRAGON?"

I turned around. Yep—a giant dragon was swimming right toward our submarine. It looked like it was going to breathe fire on us any second!

CHAPTER ELEVEN
Intel from Durga the Robot

I scrambled backward, waiting for the hot flames. But the dragon didn't breathe fire at me. It just peered at us through the window. It probably wasn't giant either. It was just that we were shrunken, I remembered. My heart was still beating wildly, though.

"What is that?" I asked.

"Durga can tell us," Professor Cheetah said. "Oh yes, here's the remote control for her."

The remote control was too big for us to pick

up now, but Professor Cheetah grinned her toothy cheetah grin and pounced onto the remote. Durga the Robot seemed to wake up. She walked stiffly on her metal legs over to the control panel, and then raised one of her ten arms, which scanned the creature outside.

"Life-form identified," Durga said. "Ruby sea dragon, a type of fish that resembles a sea horse, although it grows much larger—to about eighteen inches. It lives off the shores of Australia, at depths too deep for most divers. Which is why it has only been captured on camera by underwater robots."

Robots like Durga, I guessed. But there was something strange about what she had said.

"Why's it called a ruby sea dragon?" I asked. "It looks brown!"

Durga continued in her robot voice. "On land the creature is a very bright red. However, down here in its natural habitat, most red light is absorbed at these depths. The color helps it to blend into the surroundings."

"This is so . . . ," Jonah said.

I dared him with my eyes to say it was *weird*. But he didn't.

"Cool!" he finished instead. "First we saw a blue dragon. Now a ruby sea dragon."

"The leafy sea dragon and weedy sea dragon,"

Durga said, "are similar creatures that also live off the coast of Australia, but at shallower depths."

Wow. I ran for the diving suits in the back. "We've got to go see them."

Professor Cheetah licked her paws. "Remember what Durga said? This is too deep for our diving suits. Besides, we need to get going to the hydrothermal vents."

I crossed my arms. "We'll never get a chance like this again. We need to go swimming with sea dragons!"

CHAPTER TWELVE
Swimming with Sea Dragons

Professor Cheetah was being a grouch about us not heading straight to the vents, but Abu, Jonah, and I put on the diving suits and went for a swim in the shallower area where the weedy and leafy sea dragons were supposed to live. We couldn't dive where the ruby sea dragon lived, but here there were other divers. Of course, it might be awkward if they spotted us, since we were all so small. Would they think we were a new species of fish?

Professor Cheetah didn't want to get her fur wet, so she stayed on the sub. So did Fluff Monster.

"Don't take too long!" she said through the communication system installed in the diving helmets.

"Don't ruin our fun!" I said back.

We were surrounded by colorful sea anemones and sea cucumbers and sea urchins. Some sea stars, too. We wandered through a kelp forest. Tropical fish swam around us. Since we were so small, a lot of them were bigger than us. Even though they were really pretty, I didn't exactly want to get mistaken for fish food. Luckily, most of the fish seemed to think we were too strange to nibble on. Our diving helmets probably didn't look like tasty treats!

"Look!" Jonah said, pointing.

But I didn't see anything. "Where?"

He pointed at the swaying seaweed. The ocean was making it move back and forth like it was blowing in the wind. But then a green-and-yellow creature came out of the leaves. It was so beautiful! Like the ruby sea dragon, it resembled a sea horse, but it had what looked like big leafy branches poking out from its body instead of legs or arms. They were like really fancy fins, or maybe feathery wings.

It must be the leafy sea dragon, and camouflaging with the kelp was its superpower!

"Wow," I said. "It blends in perfectly with the seaweed."

"That thing can really sneak up on you," Jonah agreed.

"Well," said Professor Cheetah in her know-it-all voice through the comm system, "they're not very good swimmers. Those leafy-looking parts aren't for swimming, but they do help them drift and sway with the ocean current. They also have small clear fins that let them swim a little but they're pretty slow."

"Hopefully they're easy to tame," I said, swimming over the sea dragon's back and then catching hold of its leafy mane. "Look, I'm riding a dragon! I'm riding a dragon! I'm queen of the world!"

Of course, I wasn't really queen of the world, or even queen of this sea dragon. It was just floating along with the water, and probably barely noticed me. But two more leafy sea dragons appeared in the kelp, and soon we were all catching a ride.

"Woo-hoo!" said Abu, holding tightly to his sea dragon.

"This is amazing!" Jonah said, bouncing in the waves over his.

The current carried us deeper into the kelp forest, where thick stalks of green kelp and seagrass surrounded us. Then I spotted something in the seagrass and weeds on the seafloor.

"Look, there's the weedy sea dragon!" I pointed.

It was orange and red and had bits of pretty purple all over it.

"Um, let's get out of here!" Abu said, sounding really scared.

"Why?" I asked. "It won't hurt us, just like the leafy ones."

"Not that," Jonah said, his voice trembling. "That!"

I looked where he pointed, and finally spotted what they were talking about. It looked like a jellyfish, but scarier than most of the ones I had seen. Its head was square and its tentacles were long and creepy, and it was swimming right toward us!

CHAPTER THIRTEEN
Tiny Harpoons of Death

I let go of my sea dragon and started swimming as fast as I could back toward the submarine. Jonah was right behind me, but Abu couldn't keep up.

"I can't swim that fast!" he cried, his arms flailing wildly.

I turned around, grabbed his hand, and kicked harder toward our sub. But it was slow going with the two of us.

Jonah noticed and swam back to take Abu's other hand. I was glad for his help—even though

I was a little surprised that Jonah could ever be helpful. With the three of us kicking, we started moving faster, but that weird square-head thing was still after us.

"Professor Cheetah, what the heck is that thing?" I asked over the comm system.

"It's a sea wasp, also called a box jelly. And you don't want to get hugged by one!" she answered. "Watch out—they're good swimmers too!"

Professor Cheetah swung the submarine back toward us, and we managed to grab on to

the front window. She took us up to the surface, where we could reenter the submarine through the hatch on top. The sea wasp seemed to be following us. I'd never seen jellyfish do that—they usually just floated along with the water, like the sea dragons had.

"Ack! It's so creepy! Are those eyes?" I asked, banging on the hatch frantically.

"Yes, it can see and it can hunt for prey," Professor Cheetah said, throwing the hatch open.

The sea wasp was really near us now.

Abu had that look on his face. The one that said he wanted to touch something he really shouldn't.

"Don't even think of getting near it," I said.

"It will sting you?" he asked.

"Each of those tentacles is covered with stinging cells that are like tiny harpoons filled with toxins," Professor Cheetah said. "It can kill us easily even when we're our regular size. Right now? There's no chance we'd survive."

Jonah shuddered. "Let's get inside, then."

CHAPTER FOURTEEN
Stars in the Dark

Fluff Monster greeted us with drool showers again.

"At least most of the drool got on my diving suit," I said, pulling it off—just in time for Fluff Monster to give me another full-body lick! Yuck!

After drenching us all with her drooly love, she caught sight of the sea wasp still swimming outside the front window. She hopped onto the control panel and started growling at it. She didn't notice or care about the buttons that controlled the sub, but her paws randomly hit some anyway, and we started rocketing off. Fluff gave one more fierce woof at the sea wasp, as if to say, *And stay out!*

"Hey," Professor Cheetah muttered as she pounced first up to the pilot's seat and then to the control panel. "I'm driving, not you!"

Cheetahs really knew how to jump—there was no way I could have gone from the floor of the submarine all the way up to the control panel in just two leaps. Fluff was satisfied that the sea wasp was gone, so she hopped back to the ground while Jonah, Abu, and I scrambled up. It was kind of like rock climbing—you just had to use whatever you could find for the next foothold.

"Now let's stop wasting time and get to a hydrothermal vent!" Professor Cheetah said. "There are some near Antarctica, and you won't believe what's down there."

"Ooh, we're going to Antarctica?" I said. "Just like Neela Phua!"

"Your aunt went to Antarctica?" Jonah asked.

"Mrs. Drake said mostly only scientists go there and it's so cold that you could get frostbite if you drop your mitten."

"Yes, Neela Phua said that too!" I said.

He started asking me lots of questions about her work, and I told him all the stuff I'd learned from her. Like how icefish there had special proteins that could keep them from freezing, unlike humans. He seemed impressed, and it was almost like I was talking to a friend. But could I really be friends with Jonah? So far he'd been acting so different during our submarine adventure than he normally did at school. He had even helped Abu and me when we were swimming away from the sea wasp. Still, I didn't know how much I could trust him.

We sat down on the front window sill as Professor Cheetah plunged the submarine into the deep. As we got farther and farther down, the waters got darker and darker. We started to see new kinds of fish and jellyfish—the kind that flickered with glowing parts.

"Ooh, bioluminescent creatures," Jonah said. "So cool."

I nodded. We'd learned the word "bioluminescent" in Mrs. Drake's lessons about the ocean. As we got even deeper, it was as dark as night outside. It looked like we were in space, surrounded by stars. Only, they weren't stars. They were the creatures that had adapted to the darkness of the deep ocean by making lights in their own bodies. Like their own built-in night-lights!

"I'm hungry!" Abu whined.

"How can you think about food at a time like this?" I asked.

"Because Professor Cheetah shrank my string cheese!" he pouted.

But I couldn't focus on snacks when something super scary-looking was coming right at us. "Ack! What the heck is that?"

CHAPTER FIFTEEN
Spooky-Fish Contest

A very creepy fish that looked like an alien stared at us through the windshield. The lights of the submarine didn't go far down here, so we could only see creatures that came close. And boy, was it close. It was probably only three inches long, but it looked plenty big to our shrunken selves. It had the long body of an eel and big black eyes. But the thing I noticed most was its big frowning mouth with sharp, spiky teeth that sparkled like diamonds.

Durga the Robot came over to inspect. "Life-form identified. The deep-sea dragonfish has teeth made of tiny crystals that are stronger than the teeth of a piranha or a shark."

"Wow!" I said.

"Cool!" Jonah said.

"Spooky!" Abu added.

It *was* pretty spooky.

Then an even bigger and scarier fish swam in front of us. It had long glowing tendrils floating around it. On top of its head, there was something sticking out that was also glowing. Like it had a lantern hanging in front of it. Those glowing parts were kind of pretty, but its face was not. It had a huge mouth that took up most of its wrinkled black face, and giant fang teeth. It looked like a monster about to swallow you.

"Life-form identified," Durga said. "This is a type of deep-sea anglerfish. They have a lure on top of their heads that may be used to attract mates or prey."

The dragonfish swam near the anglerfish. In

a flash the anglerfish's huge jaw chomped it right up, whole!

"Scary!" Abu said.

"Gross!" I said.

"Cool!" Jonah said.

I grinned at Jonah. "It's gross but also cool. That lure on its head is definitely a smart invention."

"It's not an invention," Professor Cheetah said bossily. "It's evolution. Over millions of years creatures evolve to survive in their environments."

That made me think about Jonah. Maybe him being mean at school was some kind of adaptation? Did he say all those mean things because he was worried about getting swallowed whole by other kids?

Not that it made what he'd said to me okay.

"Still think it's an insult to come from the bottom of the sea?" I asked him.

He looked embarrassed, so he definitely remembered his rude comments from my presentation.

"I guess the bottom of the sea is pretty—aaack!"

Jonah screamed as yet another sea monster came our way. It had long whiskers, a dragon-like face, and a long red fin that ran all the way down the length of its huge back. This wasn't like the dragonfish or the anglerfish. It didn't just look big because we were little. It was actually gigantic! As it wiggled by, it slammed against our sub, and everything shook. I stumbled backward.

"Life-form identified," Durga said. The robot didn't seem bothered by the shaking of the submarine. "Giant oarfish. They are filter feeders that eat small plankton and are generally not dangerous to humans, but they may have inspired old sea monster legends. Oarfish can grow quite large, often about ten to fifteen feet. And much bigger giant oarfish have been reported. They've only very rarely been spotted alive, and we don't know exactly how big they can grow."

All I knew was that this one was probably twice as long as the submarine. It slammed against us again. So much for not being dangerous to humans!

Jonah bumped into me. So did Abu. We were falling—all over the buttons on the control panel. And the submarine started zigzagging this way and that. We were out of control!

CHAPTER SIXTEEN
Black Smokers

Arf! Arf! Arf!" Fluff Monster barked as she went sliding across the submarine.

Professor Cheetah jumped onto the buttons to regain control. *Pounce, pounce, pounce.* We managed to whiz away from the oarfish. But Fluff Monster had had enough of all those strange alien creatures that were down here. She started barking at every single fish that swam by. Professor Cheetah plunged us even deeper.

There was a loud creaking on the submarine.

"What is that?" I asked.

"It's scary!" Abu said, hugging me.

I thought Jonah would make fun of us. But it creaked again, and then he hugged us too. "What's happening?"

"Don't worry," Professor Cheetah said. "There's so much heavy water above us that the submarine is moaning a little. But we're safe. I'm sure the submarine is strong enough. I did all the calculations."

"What if you messed up carrying the three again?" I asked.

"That only happened one time!" Professor Cheetah said.

"And because of that, we're all shrunk and we can't get unshrunk!" I reminded her.

"We're going to get unshrunk." Professor Cheetah's whiskers twitched. "Look, we've made it to the hydrothermal vents near Antarctica! Powerful energy, here we come!"

We all climbed back up onto the control panel. Our submarine's headlights showed what looked

like big tall columns of black smoke coming out of the ground.

"Cool! I didn't know you could have smoke underwater!" Jonah said, pressing his nose against the window.

Professor Cheetah pounced onto another button. "What we're seeing is called a black smoker—but it's not actually smoke. There's a crack in the seafloor, and magma from Earth's crust heats up the water inside the crack. It's like a pot of boiling water, and when things get hot enough, the

water comes exploding out, along with a bunch of chemicals and minerals. When the hot stuff mixes with the cold, deep seawater, it makes these solid smoky-looking columns."

"So this is what you needed for your Unshrinker?" I asked. "Are you sure you can't just use some double-A batteries?"

"Yes, I'm sure. The energy here is much more powerful than double-A batteries!" Professor Cheetah said. "Some people have wondered if we could use these hydrothermal vents as a natural energy source instead of coal or oil. But it would be dangerous. Humans could cause all sorts of problems if they tried it, but as a cheetah, I know to only use it for special occasions—like right now."

"So let's go!" I said, grabbing my diving suit.

"No, we can't go out there." Professor Cheetah's whiskers twitched. "The water is too hot near the vent. Too cold everywhere else. Plus, like I said, the water pressure could crush your bones. But Durga can go."

CHAPTER SEVENTEEN
Ghost in the Water

Durga left through a double-door system. We couldn't open the top hatch or we'd get flooded! But if you have two doors, you can step in between them. Then when you open the outside door, just leave the inner door closed to keep water from getting into the submarine!

Soon Durga was outside with the Unshrinker. The robot had a camera and sent close-up images back to the submarine. We could see that she was stepping through a bunch of living creatures.

There were tons of sea anemones and barnacles covering the area around the vent.

"Scientists were surprised when they found life at the bottom of the sea," Professor Cheetah said. "It's actually very interesting. You know how plants convert sunlight into energy?"

"Yeah," I said, remembering learning about it in school. "They use photosynthesis."

"Plants make their food from sunlight," Jonah added.

Professor Cheetah nodded. "Yes, exactly. And some animals eat those plants for energy. Some other animals and humans eat plants and animals. But none of that would be possible without sunlight. Sunlight feeds most of the ecosystems on land and in the upper parts of the ocean."

I nodded. "But there's no sunlight this deep. So how can there be any living creatures down here?"

"The scientists who came down here were confused by that at first, too." Professor Cheetah's tail flicked. "But they discovered tiny living creatures that can convert the chemicals coming out of the vents into their food. They're called chemosynthetic bacteria because they get their energy from chemicals."

"Weird," Jonah said.

I raised my eyebrows.

"But cool," he finished.

I nodded. "Very cool. But there's a lot more down here than just bacteria! Look at those cool sea anemones and sea stars and all that other stuff!"

"You're right," said Professor Cheetah. "Some of the larger creatures feed on the chemosynthetic bacteria. Other creatures eat those, and then even bigger creatures feed on those."

I understood now. "So even though most of the life on land is powered by the sun, the ecosystem down here is powered by the energy and chemicals from the vent!"

Jonah nodded thoughtfully. "A different kind of food chain, but it still works."

I nudged him. "The bottom of the sea is kind of amazing, huh?"

"Totally," he agreed.

Just then Durga's robot voice came through the comm system. "Life-form identified. Yeti crab."

Durga sent us a video of a mountain of crabs, piled up on top of one another. They looked cute, like stuffed animals. Durga zoomed in on one so we could see it more clearly. It had a hard shell back, but its legs and two big front arms were covered in furry creamy-white hair. It looked like it wanted to give you a big fuzzy hug. Though its claws would probably pinch.

Durga's robot voice continued. "These crabs

have gardens of chemosynthetic bacteria in their furry chests and arms that they eat."

"So cool!" Jonah said.

"So cute!" I said.

"So spooky!" Abu added.

"Woof! Woof! Woof!" barked Fluff. She probably didn't like me thinking anyone else could possibly be cute.

Then another creature caught Durga's attention as she walked on her two big mechanical legs over all the barnacles and sea anemones and mussels and sea snails and who knew what else. The camera pointed to . . . a ghost.

"Aaahh!" Abu screamed. And then he giggled. "Are we in a haunted house?"

"Seems like it," I said, shivering.

"The Deep-Sea House of Horrors!" Jonah agreed.

"Life-form identified," Durga said. "Deep-sea Antarctic octopus. Also called a 'ghost octopus,' this creature resembles other deep-sea octopuses but is white, almost clear-looking. They have been difficult to capture on camera, and not much is known about them."

We watched as the little ghost octopus scrambled across the ocean floor. It used its tentacles to waddle, but it was surprisingly fast—gone in a flash.

But I had a pretty great idea for my next Halloween costume.

Just then there was a big cloud of more hot stuff coming out of the vent. It had been leaking slowly, but now it was really smoking.

"Danger," reported Durga. "Danger. Temperature levels rising rapidly."

"Oh great, it's going to blow," Professor Cheetah said, pouncing rapidly onto the remote control buttons.

"Powering Unshrinker now." Durga pulled out an instrument and held it over the new hot minerals spewing out like a geyser. "Hydrothermal energy captured."

"Success!" Professor Cheetah said, her whiskers twitching.

Durga swam back to the submarine and into the outer hatch of the double-door system just as another big burst from the vent sent the submarine rocketing through the water. It all happened so fast that we had nothing to hold on to.

"Whoa!"

"Ouch!"

"Don't bump me!"

"Arf! Arf! Arf!"

CHAPTER EIGHTEEN
Hungry and Tired and Missing Home

Eventually Professor Cheetah got control of the submarine again. As we drifted farther away, we could still see the chemicals bursting out like a geyser.

"I hope the ghostie octopus is okay!" Abu said.

"Me too," I said. "And those yeti crabs."

"Arf! Arf! Arf!" Fluff Monster barked at the door.

"Thank you for the reminder, Fluff Monster," Professor Cheetah said. "Let's pump out the water in the double-door system so Durga can reenter."

A minute later the inside hatch opened, and there was Durga, holding the Unshrinker. But there was something wrong with the robot.

"Hey! One of her arms looks broken," I said.

"Oh no!" Professor Cheetah leaped over to inspect the damage. "Looks like some of the metal got melted in the blast. We'd better remove this arm, or it might fall off the next time Durga goes out. There's enough trash in the ocean, and we wouldn't want to add to it."

"True," I said. Mrs. Drake had told us how plastics and other trash were messing up habitats in the ocean. It was really sad.

"Unfortunately, this arm was also storing the data," Professor Cheetah added. "Our videos have been destroyed."

"The ghostie octopus video?" Abu said. "Noooooo! Now I won't be a famous scientist without it!"

He started crying. I wasn't sure if it was really because we'd lost the videos or because he was

worried about the ghost octopus. Or maybe he was just hungry for a snack—it was hard to tell with five-year-olds! Though, I also felt sad about having to say goodbye to our new deep-sea friends.

After removing Durga's broken arm, Professor Cheetah picked up the Unshrinker. She pressed some buttons but nothing happened.

"What's the matter with this thing? Why won't it work?" she muttered.

I hoped we weren't going to be stuck this small for the rest of our lives. It had been fun swimming with sea dragons and making faces at sea monsters and visiting ghosts at the bottom of the sea. But I was really starting to get hungry and tired, just like Abu was acting. Plus, I wanted to spend more time with Neela Phua and my family back on the beach.

"I want my string cheese!" Abu said, still crying. Oh boy. He was about to have a meltdown. I didn't really blame him.

"You know, I could use one too!" Jonah said, rubbing his stomach. "How long have we been out here?"

I had no idea. Imagination Fuel kind of changed how time worked in a way I didn't really understand. Otherwise we probably couldn't have taken a submarine out to Antarctica in one day.

"Aha!" Professor Cheetah said, her whiskers twitching. "I see now. The safety was on."

"Wait, why didn't you put a safety on the

Micromaker?" I asked. My mood was getting worse by the second.

"Well, I was going to, but I sort of . . . well, forgot," Professor Cheetah said. "But don't worry. I'll add it on just as soon as we're back home. Now, ready, everyone?"

She didn't wait for our answer before pulling the trigger.

KABLAM! BOOM! SHAZAM!

CHAPTER NINETEEN
Accidentally Gigantic

As Jonah, Abu, and I grew back into our regular sizes, our arms and legs bumped and tangled against one another. We were all way too big to be sitting on the control panel together.

"Whoa!"

"Ouch!"

"Get off me!"

"Arf! Arf! Arf!"

We scrambled off the panel, accidentally pushing way too many buttons as we bumped onto the floor. The submarine started to zigzag all over the place again, but Professor Cheetah got it back under control pretty quickly. Meanwhile, Fluff Monster licked my face. But this time it was just a little bit of drool, rather than an entire shower. I liked it better this way.

"Did you miss us being normal?" I asked, scratching her ears and rubbing her back. "Or did you just miss the back rubs?"

Fluff wiggled her back in a way that said she had definitely missed the back rubs.

Abu reached for the Unshrinker and pointed it at something I couldn't see.

"What are you doing?" I asked, worried about what he was up to.

KABLAM!

There was the Snack Pack.

"Yay!" Abu said. "My string cheese!"

As he reached for the snack, he dropped the Unshrinker. But this time the safety wasn't on!

"Abu, wait—"

SHAZAM!

And then Blue Boss was suddenly a huge scary dragon, way too big for its bucket. We all screamed as it seemed to reach for us. Whatever venomous sting it had when it was little would be a hundred times as powerful now that it was a giant!

CHAPTER TWENTY
Bye-Bye, Blue Boss

KABLAM!

With a flash of light, Blue Boss was back to being an inch long, flopping on the floor. Durga held the Micromaker in one of her many arms, and picked up Blue Boss with another arm. She then dropped the blue dragon gently back into its bucket.

"Oh thank goodness," I said, collapsing onto the floor. "I'm glad robots can't get stung."

Professor Cheetah grinned her toothy cheetah grin. "See? The Micromaker is fun!"

"Fun that's probably going to get us killed," I muttered.

"Hey, you wanted to be an explorer," she replied, pulling some of her favorite impala-flavored chips and hare jerky out of the Snack Pack.

Professor Cheetah was such a know-it-all. Whatever. She was still my best stuffie. And I suddenly felt like giving her a big hug. After all, we'd almost gotten attacked by a giant blue dragon! She squeezed me back, flicking her tail. Then she let Durga drive the submarine while we snacked.

I helped myself to some peanut butter crackers. Jonah was impressed by the selection inside the giant Snack Pack, and he was soon munching on a chocolate granola bar. As the submarine went back toward the surface, we started to see more and more sunshine through the water. It was like watching the sunrise, but the colors were made of pretty turquoises and teals and also gold.

Those scary deep-sea creatures were behind us, and now we started seeing more of the colorful tropical fish we were used to. A sea turtle waved at us through the window. We saw some pretty jellyfish, too, though I was glad to be away from their stingers.

Next I spotted a cool-looking blue-and-violet creature floating ahead of us, on the surface of the water. It looked like a jellyfish, with its head up top and really long tendrils floating below.

"Life-form identified," said Durga. "Portuguese man-of-war. An ocean drifter that is actually not one creature but a group of small creatures that work together like one. It's also very venomous."

"And a favorite snack for a blue dragon!" I said. "Look, Blue Boss. Are you hungry?"

Blue Boss fluttered its feathery fingers—its cerata, Neela Phua had called them. That probably meant it was definitely very hungry. We took our submarine up above the surface of the water and scrambled up the ladder and through the top hatch. I popped out first, then Abu, then Jonah.

After being in the deep dark bottom of the ocean, the sunshine felt so good on my skin. I held the bucket with Blue Boss.

"I don't want to say goodbye!" Abu cried.

"Me either," I said. "But we have to. This is Blue Boss's home."

Abu chomped on his string cheese sadly. "Bye-bye, Blue Boss."

"Bye-bye!" I said, climbing a little farther across the top of the submarine so I could reach the water. Instead of dumping Blue Boss out, I dunked the bucket into the water and the blue dragon started drifting away with the current.

I was careful to keep my hands out of the way, holding the handle of the bucket instead of the sides. "Good luck!"

I was worried about whether the little venom-stealing creature would be okay, but soon enough I saw it float toward the Portuguese man-of-war. It had no fear of the much larger creature's stings—instead it latched right on. I didn't know how long it would take to eat its prey. The waves made them drift away.

I felt a tear sliding down my cheek. I'd miss it.

CHAPTER TWENTY-ONE
Human and Puppy Adaptations

When we returned to the beach where we'd left our families, the submarine melted away and we were back on a driftwood log pushed just a little ways off the shore.

Dad waded over, waving. "You kids sure have been playing on this driftwood log for a long time! What's so interesting about it?"

Abu grinned. "We turned it into a submarine and went to the bottom of the sea!"

I knew that grown-ups didn't understand the

power of Imagination Fuel, but that was okay. Imagination Fuel was so cool that time worked differently on our submarine. Our parents had only seen us playing right here on the beach, but in the space of a blink, we'd had our whole underwater adventure.

"That sounds very interesting, Abu," Dad said. "How about you come to land and tell us all about it? Ready for some food?"

"Yes!" screamed Abu. I guessed he was still pretty hungry. He took off through the water to get back to the sand, careful to keep his Snack Pack from getting wet.

Luckily, Dad had hot dogs cooking on a park grill. They smelled amazing, and I waded over in a daze. Fluff Monster barked from behind me. She was on the log, but she was too small to wade. She'd have to swim to get back to shore.

"Come on," I said encouragingly.

Her nose twitched. Her tongue lolled out.

"You know you want a hot dog," said Jonah, waving one around for Fluff to sniff.

"Hey, you already got one?" I asked.

"Your dad handed it to me!" he said, taking a big bite. "I couldn't"—munch, munch—"say no."

Fluff Monster seemed to agree. She took a running leap from the log, then paddled her legs as hard as she could. I was so proud of her when she reached the beach.

"What a good doggie!" I said, giving her some hot dog bits for her trouble. "You're such a good doggie!"

We all sat down at the picnic table, dripping ocean water. I couldn't believe how starving I was! All those spooky sea creatures—and the beautiful ones—had kept my heart racing for most of the trip. Now I was ready to relax.

My parents, Neela Phua, and other aunts and uncles were all chatting away. Mom was talking about some new experiments in her lab, then another aunt said something about silicon chips, and then another uncle changed the subject to a new vaccine his company was making. It was the usual talk in my science-loving family.

I knew they'd never notice we were gone—they really thought we'd spent the whole morning playing on a log!

Jonah's mom came over and beamed at us. "I'm so glad you two are getting along. Jonah's always talking about how clever you are, Sejal."

I glanced at Jonah. Since when?

But his mom didn't notice my surprise, and kept talking. "He's nervous about his presentation on ocean creatures on Monday. Do you have any tips for him?"

Jonah, nervous? For real?

He turned pink. "Mom!"

I was tempted to tease him. To take his smirking power, the way Blue Boss could take the man-of-war's stinging cells.

But I wasn't Blue Boss. I was a human being, and I didn't want to adapt into a meanie.

"I was nervous too," I said instead. "Talking in front of the whole class is hard. And it's even harder when people ask questions that aren't about your project at all, but just to make fun of you."

Okay, so I wasn't going to sting him, but I wasn't just going to ignore his stings either.

Jonah ducked his head. "Sorry about that. I shouldn't have asked if you were from the bottom of the ocean. It wasn't cool."

"No, it wasn't," I agreed.

"Jonah!" his mom said. "I'm surprised at you. How could you say a thing like that?"

"I said I'm sorry." He looked like he really was. "Besides, now I know that everything at the bottom of the ocean is actually awesome. So I guess it was a compliment?"

I nudged him with my shoulder. "It better be."

He nudged me back. "You're pretty fun, Sinha. We should hang out again."

I figured it was a compliment to be called by my last name, something the boys at school did with their friends.

"You're not too bad either, Williams." I picked up Professor Cheetah and squeezed her. She was quiet now, in her normal stuffie form since there were grown-ups around. "But just so you know, if you go back to acting annoying, I'll send Professor Cheetah to eat you."

Our parents laughed. But when they weren't looking, Professor Cheetah grinned a very toothy cheetah grin. It was a bit scary. Luckily, Jonah didn't know that little boys gave her tummy troubles. And I wasn't about to tell him.

Jonah held up his hands. "Okay, okay. I don't want to get eaten. Now, do you have any other tips for the presentation?"

"Glitter," I said. "Plenty of glitter."

Jonah laughed. "Wait, are you serious?"

"It impresses teachers," I promised him.

As we talked, the sun warmed us and the food felt good in my belly. Fluff Monster brought her sparkly floating toy to me—and when I threw it for her, she actually swam out into the water to bring it back!

My silly little pup had adapted too.

Author's Note

While Sejal wouldn't actually be able to travel all over the world to see them in one day, the marine life creatures mentioned in this book are all real. Giant oarfish are so big and scary-looking that they may have inspired tales of sea monsters long ago. Blue dragons are a type of sea slug, also called a nudibranch, and can truly steal stinging cells from their prey. The leafy, weedy, and ruby sea dragons are beautiful creatures that live off the coast of Australia.

In deeper waters strange bioluminescent creatures have adapted to the cold and dark. And hydrothermal vents really do spit up gases and chemicals that bacteria can feed on way at the bottom of the ocean. The vents have their own fascinating ecosystems that scientists are still learning more about. Right now it's very difficult for humans to get down that deep, but maybe someday we'll be able to visit more easily!

These amazing habitats and creatures are definitely weird, but very cool. They're also threatened by pollution, trash, and climate change. If we want these creatures to stay safe, we need to work hard to keep the oceans clean and beautiful. Can you help by spreading the word?

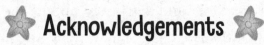 Acknowledgements

I'm so grateful to swim along through another Sejal adventure with the support of my team: my stalwart agent Penny Moore; my intrepid editor Alyson Heller; my genius illustrator Abira Das; as well as Kristin Gilson, Valerie Garfield, Anna Jarzab, Olivia Ritchie, Heather Palisi, Amelia Jenkins, Anna Elling, Bezawit Yohannes, and the teams at Aladdin and Aevitas Creative Management.

Thank you, Paul Decker, for the delightful behind-the-scenes aquarium tour, and for the early draft read—my science is better for it. My critique group remains the best school of fish to travel uncharted waters with: Flor Salcedo, S. Isabelle, Linda Cheng, Michele Bacon, and Candace Buford. Thanks, Summer, for being my youngest early draft reader—your enthusiasm means the world.

I'm grateful to my parents for fostering my

love of reading and curiosity about the world from an early age. Cleo, you're the snuggliest and most distracting writing buddy. To my husband, cheers to countless adventures, big and small.

It all started with Commander B, the dauntless cardboard box explorer in my life with an affinity for spunky cheetahs. Love you.

As always, I appreciate the parents, teachers, librarians, booksellers, and caregivers who seek out diverse reading for kids. And to my readers: Keep swimming (safely, of course)—there's so much more fabulous stuff to see and do out there!

Don't miss Sejal's next out-of-this-world adventure!

ABOUT THE AUTHOR

MAYA PRASAD is a South Asian American author, a Caltech graduate, and a former software engineer. She currently resides in the Pacific Northwest, where she enjoys hiking, kayaking, and writing stories with joyful representation for kids and teens.

The Sejal Sinha chapter book series was inspired by her own kiddo, who also has a favorite cheetah stuffie, an active imagination, and a trusty cardboard box. Visit her website MayaPrasad.com or find her on Instagram, Twitter, or TikTok @msmayaprasad.

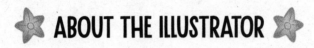

ABOUT THE ILLUSTRATOR

ABIRA DAS was born in India. As a child her biggest influences were watching her father drawing and painting and her love of Disney animation movies. Throughout the year you will find her sipping tea, bookworming, listening to music, intensely doodling while having telephonic conversations, traveling the world, expanding her collection of soft toys and action figures, binge watching anything she can, and enhancing her world of creativity.